CinderSilly

- Dedicated to making the best of it and finding the best along the way.
To Betty, Audrey and Michael who do it everyday.
– Diana

- To the ever-inspiring Ivy Bee.
– Jill and Thom

- To families everywhere who pull together to make life fun.
- Alice

Acknowledgements:
For all the visionaries who have supported Dramatic Adventures' programs, materials and the development of CinderSilly. You know who you are. Thank you.

Text copyright: © 2011 Diana B. Thompson
Art copyright: © 2011 Dramatic Adventures, Inc.
Lyrics copyright: © 2011 Alice Becker

Summary: In this variation of Cinderella,
CinderSilly learns to make chores fun,
and magic is in the power of imagination.

ISBN-13: 978-0-9847 351-0-5

Book Design: Jill Haller / Thom Buchanan
Contributing Designer: Katie Jennings
Editor: Theresa Howell
Educational Consultant: Betty J. Brittain, Ed.D.
Inspiration & model for CinderSilly: Audrey Thompson

Proudly printed in the USA by
        Worzalla
Stevens Point, Wisconsin 54481

10 9 8 7 6 5 4 3 2 1
First Printing

For more information about CinderSilly,
Dramatic Adventures' products and programs,
parent and teacher support, visit:

www.dramaticadventures.com

CinderSilly

WRITTEN BY **Diana B. Thompson**

ILLUSTRATED BY **Jill Haller** AND **Thom Buchanan**

Dramatic

Once upon a time,
there lived a girl named Cinderella.
She shared a home with her stepmother
and two stepsisters. It was a time when folks
raised cows and chickens for their milk and eggs.
They washed clothes by hand and traveled
down bumpy roads. Cinderella's family
had maids to do the hard chores,

until...

. . . the money ran out.

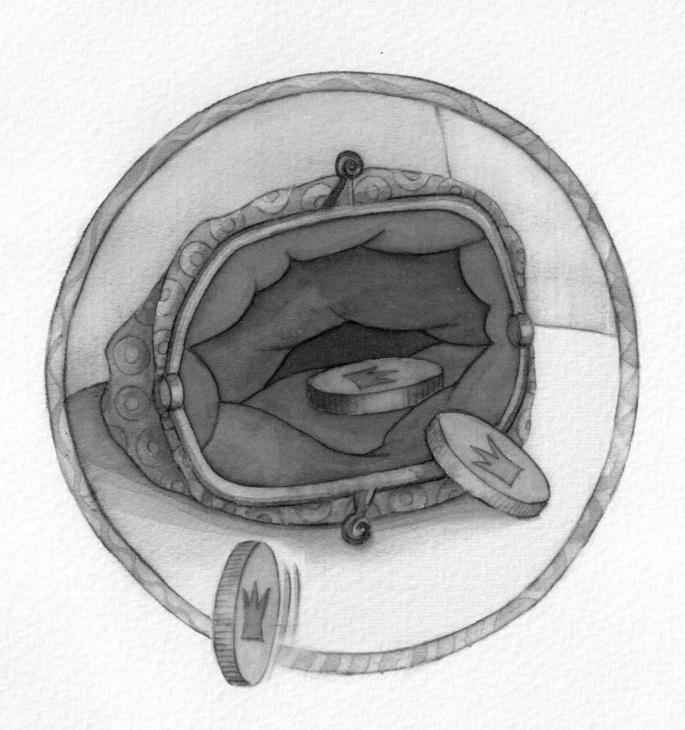

Her stepmother moaned miserably, "Life is a chore, a very hard chore."
Everyone agreed, everyone except Cinderella.
"Maybe chores can be fun," she said hopefully.

"Let's make the best of it."

"Work is no fun Cinderella, that's ridiculous," her stepmother
grumbled. "Go milk the cows all by yourself. Then you'll see."

Cinderella took the milk pails and walked slowly to the barn. Cows are big, and this was a very big chore. The first cow would not stand still. After several tries, Cinderella began to feel frustrated.

"Perhaps if I make up a song it will help me along." She began to sing.

♪ "Any chore can be made fun, tra-la-la-la day-o. ♪
I'll milk the cows in the morning sun, tra-la-la-la day-o."

squish squirt
squish squirt

Why, the cows had never heard singing.
They became quiet and still. Suddenly the milk splashed into the pail
faster and faster. Cinderella pulled and pushed and pumped her hands
up and down, up and down. The beating sound of the *squish squirt,*
squish squirt played a steady rhythm as she sang.

Cinderella's stepsisters were spying from behind the door. One giggled, "Cinderella is so silly. She is singing to the cows!" The other squealed, "Let's call her CinderSilly!"

Cinderella did not like their teasing, and tried hard not to listen. She filled ten pails with milk, more delicious and refreshing than ever.

Cinderella's stepmother asked, "Now you agree that life is a chore, don't you?"
Cinderella replied, "Sometimes I think life is just what you make it. So I made the chore more fun."

Clearly Cinderella had not learned her lesson.
Her stepmother was not pleased. "Cinderella, go wash the clothes. It will be hard work, but it's for your own good."

Cinderella walked to the well. She filled bucket after bucket with water and loaded the tub. She scrubbed the clothes on a washboard. It was hard work. After awhile, Cinderella felt discouraged.

"I know!" Cinderella cried.
"I'll make bubbles while I wash the clothes," and she jumped in the tub.
With a twist, a turn and a twirl, a chorus of soapsuds filled the air.
bubble pop,
bubble bubble, pop pop.

"Any chore can be made fun,
tra-la-la-la day-o.
Wash the clothes for everyone,
tra-la-la-la day-o."

bubble pop

bubble bubble pop

pop

bubble
bubble

pop

pop

Cinderella's stepsisters were watching.
"CinderSilly is dancing with the clothes! She's ridiculous!"
they laughed. Cinderella played along. She sang louder,
spun faster, and looked even sillier than before.

When she was through, Cinderella was tired but cheerful. The whites were whiter and the colors were brighter than ever.

Her stepmother was furious. "Cinderella, you're not learning! Now go collect the eggs all by yourself," she ordered.

Cinderella opened the gate to the chicken pen and stepped inside.
Chickens picked and pecked and poked at her feet. She wanted to
kick and scream!

flip flap flop

flip

flap

flop

Instead, she took a deep breath.
She watched the chickens prance and
dance. Cinderella bent her arms like
wings. She marched through the yard
with a flip flap flop as she sang.

"Any chore can be made fun,
tra-la-la-la day-o.
Pick the eggs up one by one,
tra-la-la-la day-o."

The stepsisters spied on Cinderella.
"Now CinderSilly is a chicken!"
they howled.

Cinderella turned toward them.
With a playful grin, she squeaked
and squawked and chased them
right through the yard.

"Any chore can be made fun,
    tra-la-la-la day-o.
Play a game of chicken run,
    tra-la-la-la day-o."

Suddenly, Cinderella's stepmother screamed out with excitement.
"Girls! We have an invitation to the castle ball!"
"A ball! Kickball or game of catch?" Cinderella asked.
"Not a ball you kick or throw, CinderSilly, it's a fancy dance,"
her stepsisters chuckled. "What will we wear?" Cinderella wondered.

"You can stay *here*.
There's too much
work to do. Maybe now
you will understand,"
snapped her stepmother.

That night, and throughout the next day, Cinderella worked very hard to finish her chores. She tried to sing, but her heart wasn't in it. She helped her stepsisters get ready for the ball and slumped in a chair as they rode away.

"Maybe life
is nothing but a chore,"
she sighed, feeling sad
and sorry for herself.
"Only magic can help
me now." She waited
and waited. Waiting
for magic is such a chore,
she waited and waited
and waited some more.

Nothing happened!

Until . . .

She picked herself up and pushed right through the door.

She ran to see a neighbor nearby.

This kind lady
was a dear
old family friend.
She had a most
unusual name.
"Hello, Princess,"
Fairy said.
"I need your help,"
Cinderella told her.
"I want to go
to the ball."
With a wave
of her spoon,
Fairy invited her in.

Fairy took Cinderella to a small room with a large trunk. Inside lay the most beautiful dress Cinderella had ever seen. It was dazzling. A long flowing skirt swung with a *swish, swish, swoosh.* Fairy pulled ribbons from a crisp, clean box. It held a pair of shiny glass slippers.

"Perfect!" Cinderella squealed.

swish swish swoosh
swish swish swoosh

"Except...

I can't stand or walk or dance in these.
Wearing glass slippers is an awful chore."

But then, she had an idea. She pulled
ribbons from the box and laced them
through her own favorite shoes.
"Like magic," Fairy smiled.

"These dancing shoes can't be broken,
and neither can a girl who is true to herself."

"Your carriage awaits."

"Oh, thank you!" Cinderella cried.

"You best be home by midnight," Fairy warned.

"That's when the sparkle wears off of every good party."

Cinderella promised, and off she dashed to the castle on the hill.

Cinderella slipped into the ballroom.
The music was playing, but no one
was having any fun at all. She didn't
want to seem out of place. So, she stood
against the wall and stared at her shoes.

The prince moaned
miserably.
"Balls are such a chore," he said.

Cinderella didn't know much about dancing, but she knew quite a lot about chores. She walked to the center of the room and began to sing.

"Any chore can be made fun, tra-la-la-la day-o,
Come and join in everyone, tra-la-la-la day-o."

Cinderella began to dance. She pulled and pumped her hands up and down like she was milking a cow. With a twist, a turn and a twirl, she moved like she was washing clothes.

bubble pop pop

swish swish swoosh

flip flap flop

flip flap flop

swish swish swoosh

bubble pop pop

swish swish swoosh

squish squirt squish squirt

Then she bent her arms like wings.
Cinderella pranced like a funky
chicken to a symphony of sounds.
flip flap flop,
bubble bubble, pop pop,
swish, swish, swoosh.
Soon everyone was dancing
and having a marvelous time.

Until . . .

. . . the clock struck midnight.

Cinderella remembered her promise.
She dashed out the door, leaving one shoe behind.

Early the next morning, a fancy footman arrived.
"Who, oh, who fits this shoe?" he asked.

"That's not mine," one stepsister replied.
"It's too ridiculous for me," said the other.
"That's my shoe," Cinderella said.

To everyone's surprise, the prince stepped forward.

"You changed everything,"
the prince said.
"Sometimes life is just what
you make it," Cinderella smiled.
"Call me CinderSilly.
Now, let's go have a ball."

And they all lived HAPPIER ever after.

Except...

. . . for the stepmother.
Her life was a chore,
a
very
hard
chore.

CinderSilly
Chore School

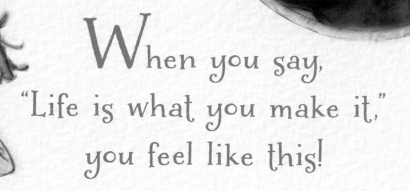

W hen you say, "Life is a chore," you feel like this.

Stepmother expects life to be hard so she makes things harder than they need to be. She could learn a lot from CinderSilly.

W hen you say, "Life is what you make it," you feel like this!

It's like saying, "I can do it!" When you change what you think and say, it affects what you feel and do. It gives you more energy to get the job done.

Look through the story and find all the ways CinderSilly makes chores fun. Can you make your chores fun too? Sing, dance and play along the way!

When you are true to yourself, you think for yourself.

Just like choosing shoes
for the dance, decide
what is right for you!

Some chores are very hard.

Use your imagination to make chores fun.
Bright ideas may be just the magic you need.
By turning work into play, you put more fun
into your day.

A special CinderSilly surprise
awaits you at
www.CinderSilly.com